P9-CQQ-941
Little Golden Books
Little Golden Books
Little Golden Books
Little Golden Books
Little Golden Books

a Little Golden Book® Collection

A GOLDEN BOOK • NEW YORK

www.goldenbooks.com
www.randomhouse.com/kids
Educators and librarians, for a variety of teaching tools, visit us at www.randomhouse.com/teachers
Library of Congress Control Number: 2007937195
ISBN: 978-0-375-87495-6
PRINTED IN CHINA
Book design by Roberta Ludlow
10 9 8 7 6 5 4 3
First Random House Edition 2008

Random House Children's Books supports the First Amendment and celebrates the right to read.

Contents

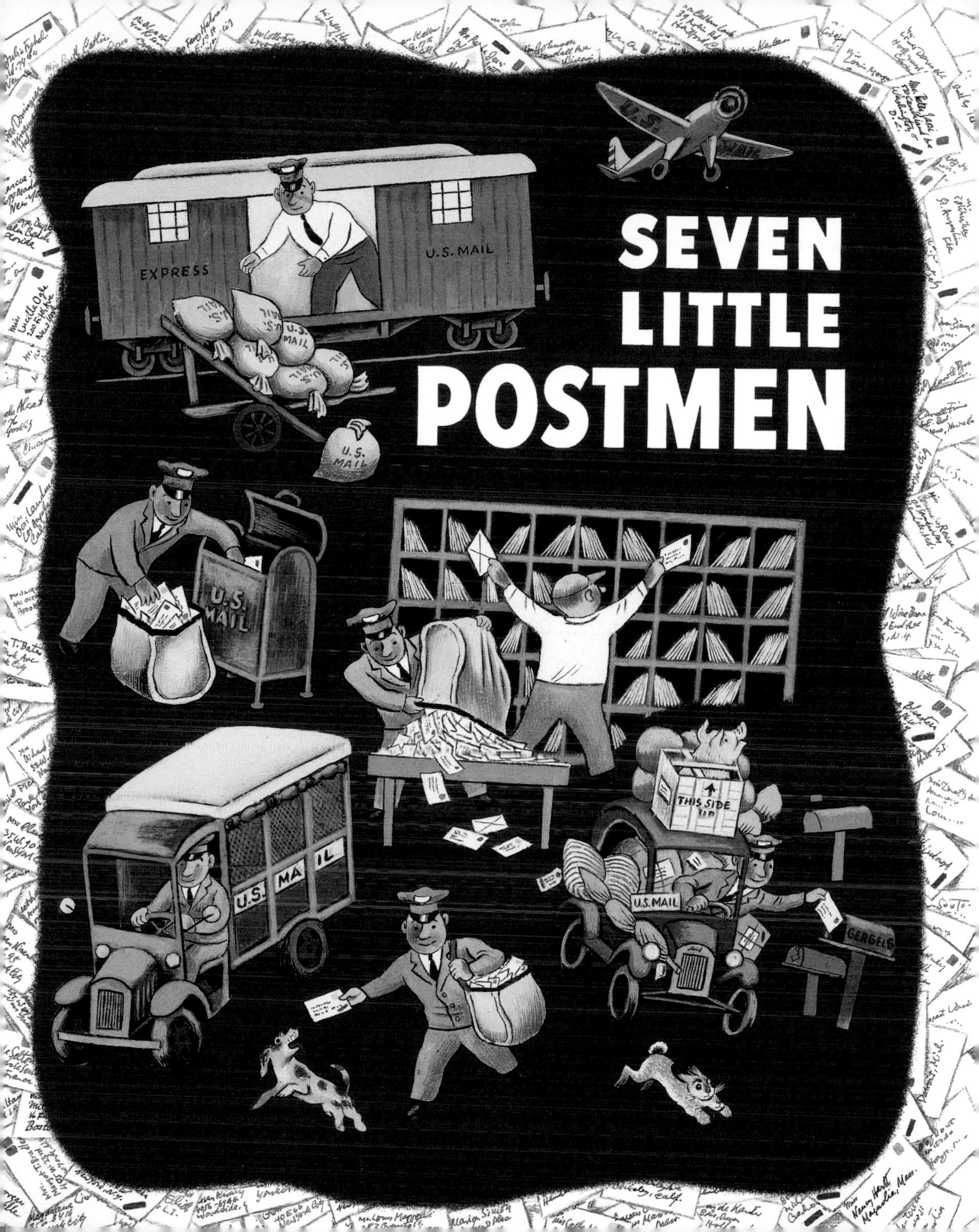
SEVEN LITTLE POSTMEN
EXPRESS
U.S. MAIL
U.S. MAIL
U.S. MAIL
U.S. MAIL
THIS SIDE UP
U.S. MAIL
GERGELY

A boy had a secret. It was a surprise.
He wanted to tell his grandmother.
So he sent his secret through the mail.
The story of that letter
Is the reason for this tale
Of the seven little postmen who carried the mail.

Because there was a secret in the letter
The boy sealed it with red sealing wax.
If anyone broke the seal
The secret would be out.

He slipped the letter into the mail box.

The first little postman
Took it from the box,
Put it in his bag,
And walked seventeen blocks
To a big Post Office
All built of rocks.

The letter with the secret
Was dumped on a table
With big and small letters
That all needed the label
Of the big Post Office.

Stamp stamp, clickety click,
The machinery ran with a quick sharp tick.
The letter with the secret is stamped at last
And the round black circle tells that it passed
Through the cancelling machine
Click whizz fast!

Big letters
Small letters
Thin and tall—
The second little postman
Sorts them all.
The letters are sorted
From East to West
From North to South.

"And this letter
Had best go West,"
Said the second
Little postman,
Scratching his chest.
Into the pouch
Lock it tight
The secret letter
Must travel all night.

The third little postman in the big mail car
Comes to a crossroad where waiting are
A green, a yellow, and a purple car.
They all stop there. There is nothing to say.
The mail truck has the right of way!
"The mail must go through!"

Up and away through sleet and hail
This airplane carries the fastest mail.
The pilot flies through whirling snow
As far and as fast as the plane can go.

The mail is landed for the evening train.
Now hang the pouch on the big hook crane!
The engine speeds up the shining rails
And the fourth little postman
Grabs the mail with a giant hook.

The train roars on
With a puff and a snort
And the fourth little postman
Begins to sort.

The train carries the letter
Through gloom of night
In a mail car filled with electric light

To a country postman
By a country road
Where the fifth little postman
Is waiting for his load.

The mail clerk
Heaves the mail pouch
With all his might
To the fifth little postman
Who grabs it tight.

Then off he goes
Along the lane
And over the hill
Until
He comes to a little town
That is very small—
So very small
The Post Office there
Is hardly one at all.

The sixth little postman
In great big boots
Sorts the letters
For their various routes—
Some down the river,
Some over the hill.

But the secret letter
Goes farther still.

The seventh little postman on R.F.D.
Carries letters and papers, chickens and fruit
To the people who live along his route.

There were parts
For a tractor

And a wig for an actor

And a funny post card
For a little boy
Playing in his own backyard.

There was something for Sally
And something for Sam

And something for Mrs. Potter
Who was busy making jam.

There were dozens of chickens
For Mrs. Pickens

And a dress for a party
For Mrs. McCarty.

At the last house along the way sat the grandmother of the boy who had sent the letter with the secret in it. She had been wishing all day he would come to visit. For she lived all alone in a tiny house and sometimes felt quite lonely.

The postman blew his whistle and gave her the letter with the red sealing wax on it—the secret letter!

"Sakes alive! What is it about?"
Sakes alive! The secret is out!
What does it say?

THAT I'M COMING TO VISIT ON SATURDAY.
MY CAT HAS SEVEN KITTENS AND I AM BRINGING
ONE TO YOU FOR YOUR VERY OWN KITTEN.
THE POSTMAN IS MY FRIEND.
YOUR GRANDSON
THOMAS
P3-109

SEVEN LITTLE POSTMEN

Seven Little Postmen carried the mail
Through Rain and Snow and Wind and Hail
Through Snow and Rain and Gloom of Night

Seven Little Postmen
Out of sight.
Over Land and Sea
Through Air and Light
Through Snow and Rain
And Gloom of Night—
Put a stamp on your letter
And seal it tight.

Pussy Willow

Once there was a little pussycat not much bigger than a pussy willow. He was just as soft and gray and furry as those little flowers clinging to the branches all about him in the early spring. So he named himself Pussy Willow.

It was a wild green world that he was born into. A forest of wildflowers grew above him. Some things were bigger than he was. And some things were smaller than he was. And he wondered at such little things.

Suddenly a bug jumped out of that wild green world and up to him.

"Where are you good to bite?" asked the bug.

"Nowhere and not at all," said Pussy Willow, and he rolled the bug back in the grass with his soft fur foot.

Bright moonlight nights came down the sky. The peepers were peeping. And the tender buds and roots and wildflowers were a gentle smell on the warm night air.

A little peeper peeped out of the pond.

"How do you know it's spring?" he peeped.

"I don't," said Pussy Willow.

"When the groundhog casts his shadow
And the small birds sing
And the pussy willows happen
And the sun shines warm
And when the peepers peep
Then it is Spring."

A deer mouse came softly out of the forest and tickled Pussy Willow on the nose.

"How odd," she said. "A cat not much bigger than a mouse."

"Little fat shadow," said the mouse, "come home with me and live in my house."

"*Kerchew!*

"I am not a shadow. Shadows don't sneeze—*Kerchew!*"

Pussy Willow gave such a big sneeze that it blew the mouse over.

Time passed, hours and minutes and nights and days. And Pussy Willow grew more fur.

Wild strawberries bloomed about him.

Green grasshoppers hopped over him.

Suddenly Pussy Willow looked up.

His pussy willows were gone. Gone.

Long yellow things and little green leaves hung from the branches where his pussy willows had been.

Where had they gone?

He would go and find them.

And he would look until he found them again.

So off he went—

through moonlight
and
starlight

and thunder
and lightning

looking for his pussy willows.

He searched

through the day
and the night

and the wind
and the rain.

Spring passed. And along came the first butterfly, and bumped bang into Pussy Willow with a soft and certain bang.

"Out of my way,

"Out of my way," said the butterfly.

"Who who are you? And what are you looking for?"

Pussy Willow sat squarely on his tail.

"Pussy willows," he said.

"Did you ever see any gray fur flowers that look just like me?"

"Up in the air,

"Up in the air," said the butterfly.

"Anything that anyone would look for is up in the air."

So Pussy Willow climbed a tree and fell asleep in a bird's nest. The birds came home and found him warm and purring next to their eggs. So they sat on him too and kept him warm.

Little friendly birds came out of the eggs and grew up and learned to fly.

"Everything that anyone would ever look for is up in the sky," they sang, and flew up.

Pussy Willow climbed all around the treetops, but he never learned to fly.

One day a bee flew by. “Who are you, and where shall I sting you?”

“Don’t,” said Pussy Willow. “But tell me, did you ever see any gray fur flowers that look just like me?”

“Sassafras,” buzzed the bee. “Look in the garden.”

So Pussy Willow climbed down into a garden. And there he found cabbages and roses, scarecrows, poppies, and pink tiger lilies.

But no pussy willows.

He went up to a big fat cabbage.

"Did you ever see any little gray fur flowers that look just like me?"

But the cabbage sat there in its great green silence and never said a word.

Up popped a mole—"Anything that anyone would look for is always in a hole."

"In a carrot," said the rabbit.

"In a garden," buzzed the bee.

"In a smell," sniffed the skunk.

And the woodpecker pecked at a tree.

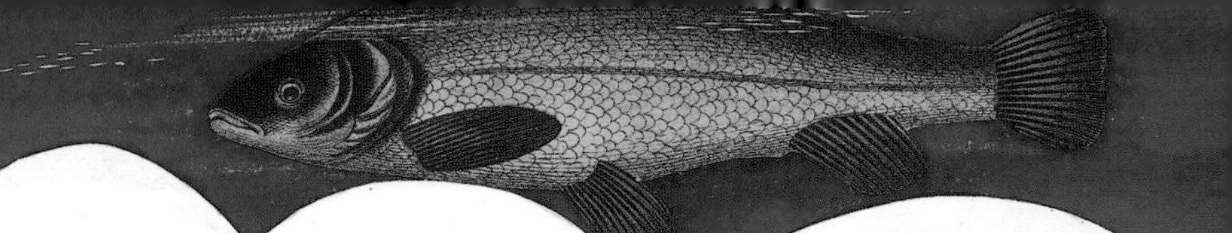

Pussy Willow hunted through moonlight and sunlight and down by the Sea. There he met an old hermit crab. The hermit crab came snapping out of his shell, waving all his claws.

"Sshhhhhhhhh!" said the hermit crab. "Why do you walk by the sea?"

"Psst," said Pussy Willow. "I walk where I please. But did you ever see any little gray fur flowers that look just like me?"

"Scuttlefish," snapped the crab. "I see that you are a pussycat, and the beach is no place for pussycats, and the sea is full of fish; and if you are looking for flowers, all the beautiful ones are in the sea."

The hermit crab snapped back into his shell and scuttled off sideways into the deep green water.

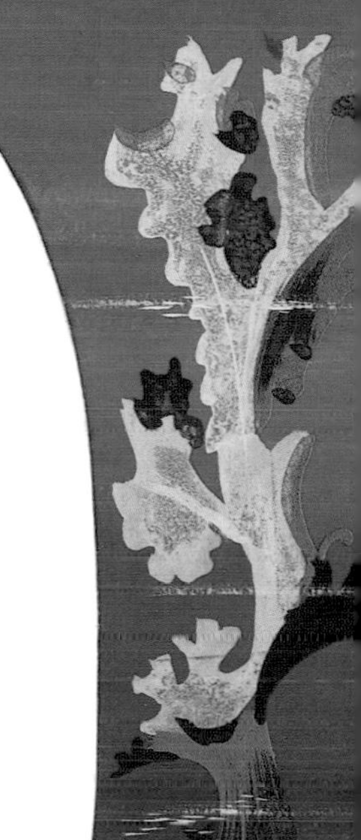

So Pussy Willow wandered through purple asters and goldenrod and pearly everlasting, through blueberries and blackberries and raspberries. But still he couldn't find his lost pussy willows.

The wind began to blow. The leaves turned red and fell from the trees. Nuts fell on Pussy Willow's head and apples dropped about him, with a loud and sudden pop.

He met a red squirrel hiding acorns.

"Are you a nut?" asked the red squirrel.

"What do you think?" said Pussy Willow. "Did you ever see a nut with whiskers and pointed ears and a switching tail?

"I am a cat looking for pussy willows. Did you ever see any little soft gray fur flowers that look just like me?"

"Go under the leaves," said the squirrel. "Everything that anyone would look for is always under the leaves."

The air grew colder. Snow fell. Pussy Willow hunted through snowstorms and black branches, and across the shining ice.

Until at last he fell asleep, a very tired pussycat under a thin branched bush. He took a little catnap. And while he was asleep something began to happen on the branches high above him.

The sun shone warm and he dreamed that there was a soft purring in the air around him.

The groundhog came out of the ground. And when he saw a little cat in his shadow—*Thump!* "Get out of my shadow," he said, and woke him up.

Then all the birds began to sing.

The red-winged blackbird, the meadowlark, and the bobolink whistled in the air.

The peepers in the pond began to peep.

It was Spring.

And when Pussy Willow uncurled himself, there were his pussy willows.

For he had fallen asleep under a pussy willow bush, and it had burst into bloom above him.

"Everything that anyone would ever look for is usually where they left it," hooted the owl.

"On a bush," sang the robin.

"In the sky," sang the lark.

"In a song
In the Spring
In the dark."

Then up popped Pussy Willow.

"Everything that anyone would ever look for is usually where they find it," purred Pussy Willow.

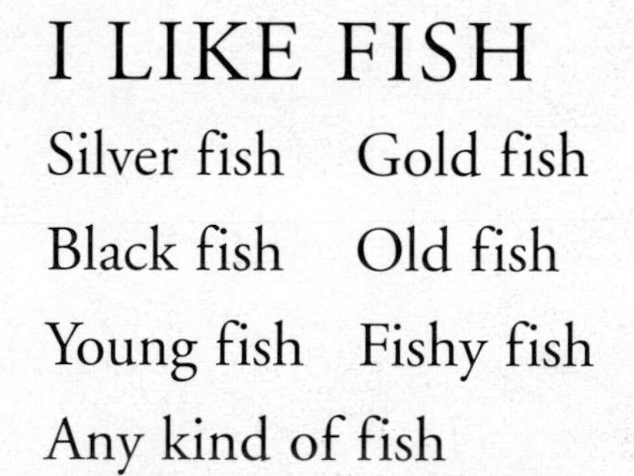

I LIKE FISH

Silver fish Gold fish
Black fish Old fish
Young fish Fishy fish
Any kind of fish

A fish in a pond
A fish in a stream
A fish in the ocean
A fish in a dream
I like fish.

THE BURGLAR IN THE DARK

One dark night the Little Fat Policeman was waiting quietly at the Police Booth. He was all alone.

Br-rr-rr rang the telephone. Someone said,

“Come fast. I think I hear a burglar prowling in my house.”

The Little Fat Policeman stuck his pistol in his holster. He grabbed his stout policeman’s billy.

Whee-ee-ee went the siren on the policeman’s little car.

Then he turned the siren off and crept silently through the night. One Little Fat Policeman!

He crept up to the house. He walked on tiptoes, creeping, creeping. He flashed his flashlight all around.

He looked in the bushes and he looked in the trees.

He patted the pistol in the holster at his side. It was there, all right. He flashed his flashlight.

But there was no burglar there.

He went in the house. He crept in the hall.

Creeping, creeping, he flashed his flashlight. But there was no burglar there.

He crept in the parlor. Creeping, creeping in the dark. He flashed his flashlight.

But there was no burglar there.

There was just a tiny little noise—a sort of scratching sound!

The Little Fat Policeman grabbed his pistol in his hand.

"Who's there?" he shouted softly.

The scratching stopped.

Instead there was a GROAN! and a SNEEZE!

The Little Fat Policeman pointed his pistol at the groan and the sneeze.

Then he flashed his flashlight—FLASH!

And suddenly there was a lot of scrambling and a barking and a whining for joy.

Because that dreadful burglar was only a—BIG WOOLLY SHEEP DOG who had lost his way.

The Little Fat Policeman laughed a big fat belly laugh, a great big warm laugh. Then he patted the woolly sheep dog, who wagged his tail and licked the Little Fat Policeman's hand.

The Little Fat Policeman put him in his car and drove him home to the right house because he knew the boy who owned him.

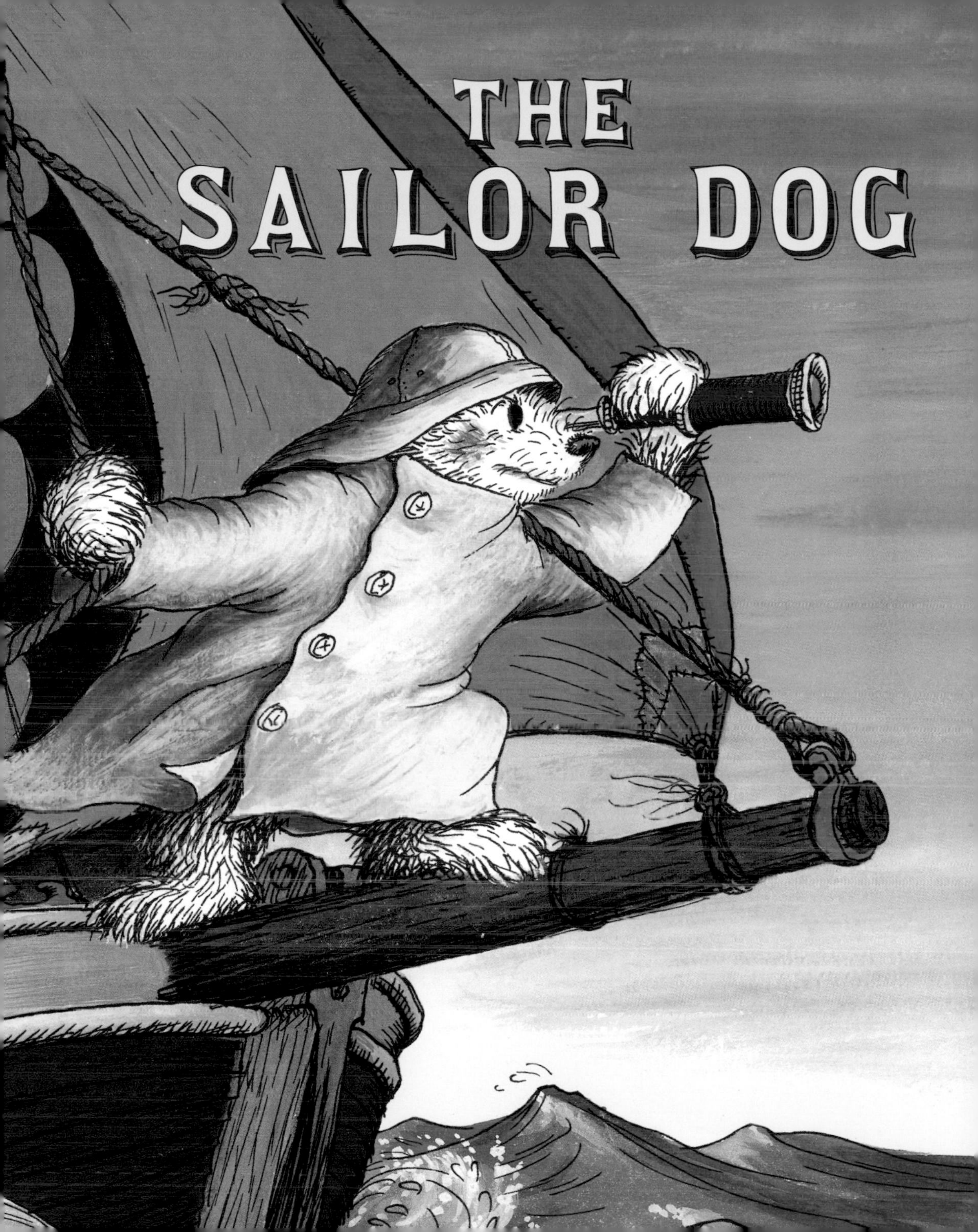
THE
SAILOR DOG

Born at sea in the teeth of a gale, the sailor was a dog. Scuppers was his name.

After that he lived on a farm. But Scuppers, born at sea, was a sailor. And when he grew up, he wanted to go to sea.

So he went to look for something to go in.

He found a little submarine. "All aboard!" they called. It was going down under the sea. But Scuppers did not want to go under the sea.

He found a little car.

"All aboard!" they called. It was going over the land. But Scuppers did not want to go over the land.

Scuppers was a sailor. He wanted to go to sea.

So Scuppers went over the hills and far away until he came to the sea.

Over the hills and far away was the ocean. And on the ocean was a ship. The ship was about to go over the sea. It blew all its whistles.

"All aboard!" they called.

"All ashore that are going ashore!"

"All aboard!"

So Scuppers went to sea.

The ship began to move slowly along. The wind blew it.

In his ship Scuppers had a little room. In his room Scuppers had a hook for his hat and a hook for his rope and a hook for his handkerchief and a hook for his pants and a hook for his spyglass and a place for his shoes and a bunk for a bed to put himself in.

At night Scuppers threw the anchor into the sea, and he went down to his little room.

He put his hat on the hook for his hat, and his rope on the hook for his rope, and his pants on the hook for his pants, and his spyglass on the hook for his spyglass, and he put his shoes under the bed and got into his bed, which was a bunk, and went to sleep.

Next morning he was shipwrecked.

Too big a storm blew out of the sky. The anchor dragged, and the ship crashed onto the rocks. There was a big hole in it.

Scuppers himself was washed overboard and hurled by huge waves onto the shore.

He was washed up onto the beach. It was foggy and rainy. There were no houses, and Scuppers needed a house.

But on the beach was lots and lots of driftwood, and he found an old rusty box stuck in the sand.

Maybe it was a treasure!

It was a treasure—to Scuppers.

It was an old-fashioned tool box with hammers and nails and an ax and a saw. Everything he needed to build himself a house. So Scuppers started to build a house, all by himself, out of driftwood.

He built a door and a window and a roof and a porch and a floor, all out of driftwood.

And he found some red bricks and built a big red chimney. And then he lit a fire, and the smoke went up the chimney.

Then the stars came out, and he was sleepy. So he built a bed of pine branches.

And he jumped into his deep green bed and went to sleep. As he slept he dreamed—

If he could build a house,
he could mend the hole in the ship.

So the next day at low tide he took his tool box and waded out and hammered planks across the hole in his ship.

At last the ship was fixed.

So he sailed away.

Until he came to a seaport in a foreign land.

By now his clothes were all worn and ripped and torn and blown to pieces. His coat was torn, his hat was blown away, and his shoes were all worn out. And his handkerchief was ripped. Only his pants were still good.

So he went ashore to buy some clothes at the Army and Navy Store. And some fresh oranges. He bought a coat. He found a red one too small. He found a blue one just right. It had brass buttons on it.

Then he went to buy a hat. He found a purple one too silly. He found a white one just right.

He needed new shoes. He found some yellow ones too small. He found some red ones too fancy. Then he found some white ones just right.

Here he is with his new hat on, and with his new shoes on, and with his new coat on, with his shiny brass buttons. (He has a can of polish and a cloth to keep them shiny.)

And he has a new clean handkerchief, and a new rope, and a bushel of oranges.

And now Scuppers wants to go back to his ship. So he goes there.

SHOE
size 8
SHOE
size5
SHOE
size 7
BRASS
POLISH

And at night when the stars came out, he took one last look through his spyglass. And went down below to his little room, and he hung his new hat on the hook for his hat, and he hung his spyglass on the hook for his spyglass, and he hung his new coat on the hook for his coat, and his new handkerchief on the hook for his handkerchief, and his pants on the hook for his pants, and his new rope on the hook for his rope, and his new shoes he put under his bunk, and himself he put in his bunk.

And here he is where he wants to be—
a sailor sailing the deep green sea.

HIS SONG

I am Scuppers the Sailor Dog—
I'm Scuppers the Sailor Dog—
I can sail in a gale
right over a whale
under full sail
in a fog.

I am Scuppers the Sailor Dog—
I'm Scuppers the Sailor Dog—
with a shake and a snort
I can sail into port
under full sail
in a fog.

The Train to TIMBUCTOO

Clackety clack—clackety clack
There was a big train

and clickety click—clickety click—clickety click
There was a very little train.

> They were on their way
> home to Timbuctoo.
> And they had just left
> the town of Kalamazoo.

Slam Bang grease the engine
throw out the throttle and give it the gun.
There was a big engineer
who drove the big engine.

And Slam Bang grease the enginc
throw out the throttle and give it the gun.
There was a little engineer
who drove the little enginc.

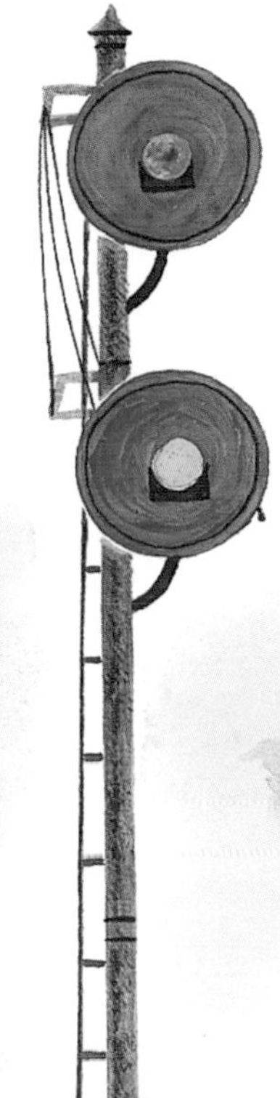

When the big engine went through a tunnel
The big engineer blew his big whistle
whoooooooooooooooooooooooooooo

When the little engine went through a tunnel
The little engineer blew his whistle
wheeeeeeeeeeeeeeeeeeeeeeeeeeeeeeeeeeeeeeeeeeeeeeeeeeeeeee

And clackety clack—clickety click
Throw out the throttle and give it the gun
whooooooooooooooooooooooooooo

wheeeeeeeeeeeeeeeeeeeeeeeeeeeeeeeeeeeeeeeeeeeeeeeeeee

Out from the big tunnel came the big engine
With the big engineer

And the big coal car

And the big baggage car

And the big passenger car

And the big dining car and the big

sleeping car and the little caboose

And then out from the little tunnel

Came the little engine
With the little engineer
And the little coal car

And the little baggage car

And the little passenger car

And the little dining car
And the little sleeping car
And the little caboose

Clickety click—clickety click

clackety clack—clackety clack

whoooooooooooooooooooooooooooooooo

wheeeeeeeeeeeeeeeeeeeeeeeeeeeeeeeeeeeeeeeeeeeeeeeeeeeeeeeeeeee

That great big train and that little tiny train
went roaring by.
Then clackety clack—clackety clack
The big train came to a big bridge
over a big river

And over the big bridge went the big engine

With
The big engineer
And the big coal car
And the big baggage car
And the big passenger car
And the big dining car
And the big sleeping car
And the little caboose

Then

Clickety click—clickety click

The little train came to a little bridge

Over a river, over a little river,

And clickety click—clickety click

Over the little bridge went the little engine

With the little engineer
And the little coal car
And the little baggage car
And the little passenger car
And the little dining car
And the little sleeping car
And the little caboose

And clickety click—clickety click

clackety clack—clackety clack—

pocketa—pocketa—pocketa—pocketa

picketa—picketa—picketa—picketa

The trains rolled on toward Timbuctoo
Far down the track from Kalamazoo
Until far away against the sky
There was a great big railroad station
And far away against the sky
There was a little railroad station.

whoooooooooo wheeeeeeeeeeeeeeeeee
As ringing their bells
dong—dong—dong ding—ding—ding
That great big train with a puff—puff—puff
And that tiny little train with a piff—piff—piff

Came home to Timbuctoo.

And if you switch
the names of the towns
in the front of the book
You can get back to
Kalamazoo.

From
Kalamazoo to Timbuctoo
It's a long way down the track
And from Timbuctoo to Kalamazoo
It's just as far to go back
From Timbuctoo to Kalamazoo
From Kalamazoo and back
A long, long way,
A long, long way,
a long way down the track.
From Kalamazoo to Timbuctoo
From Timbuctoo
and back.

THE
COLOR KITTENS

RED
YELLOW

Once there were two color kittens with green eyes, Brush and Hush. They liked to mix and make colors by splashing one color into another. They had buckets and buckets

and buckets and buckets of color to splash around with. Out of these colors they would make all the colors in the world.

The buckets had the colors written on them, but of course the kittens couldn't read. They had to tell by the colors. "It is very easy," said Brush.

"Red is red. Blue is blue," said Hush.

But they had no green. "No green paint!" said Brush and Hush. And they wanted green paint, of course, because nearly every place they liked to go was green.

Green as cats' eyes
Green as grass
By streams of water
Green as glass.

So they tried to make some green paint.

Brush mixed red paint and white paint together—and what did that make? It didn't make green.

But it made pink.

Pink as pigs

Pink as toes

Pink as a rose
Or a baby's nose.

Then Hush mixed yellow and red together, and it made orange.

Orange as an orange tree

Orange as a bumblebee

Orange as the setting sun
Sinking slowly in the sea.

The kittens were delighted, but it didn't make green.

Then they mixed red and blue together—and what did that make? It didn't make green. It made a deep dark purple.

Purple as violets

Purple as prunes

Purple as shadows
On late afternoons.

Still no green! And then . . .

O wonderful kittens! O Brush! O Hush!

At last, almost by accident, the kittens poured a bucket of blue and a bucket of yellow together, and it came to pass that they made a green as green as grass.

Green as green leaves on a tree

Green as islands in the sea.

The little kittens were so happy with all the colors they had made that they began to paint everything around them. They painted . . .

Green leaves
    and red berries
and purple flowers
    and pink cherries
Red tables
    and yellow chairs
Black trees
    with golden pears.

Then the kittens got so excited they knocked their buckets upside down and all the colors ran together. Yellow, red, a little blue, and a little black . . . and that made brown.

Brown as a tugboat

Brown as an old goat

Brown as a beaver

And in all that brown, the sun went down. It was evening and the colors began to disappear in the warm dark night.

The kittens fell asleep in the warm dark night with all their colors out of sight and as they slept they dreamed their dream—

A wonderful dream
Of a red rose tree
That turned all white
When you counted three

One . . . Two . . .

Three

Of a purple land
In a pale pink sea

Where apples fell
From a golden tree

And then a world of Easter eggs
That danced about on little short legs.

And they dreamed that
A green cat danced
With a little pink dog

Till they all disappeared in a soft gray fog.

And suddenly Brush woke up and Hush woke up. It was morning. They crawled out of bed into a big bright world. The sky was wild with sunshine.

The kittens were wild with purring and pouncing—

They got so pouncy they knocked over the buckets and all the colors ran out together.

There were all the colors in the world and the color kittens had made them.

Selections from

The GOLDEN BUNNY

THE GOLDEN BUNNY

O best loved Bunny in all the world, this is the story of you.

Far off in a far country in a green green wood greener than most woods in this world, a Bunny opened his eyes.

He saw the winds blowing the ferns far above him and he never had heard of a tree.

Little shiny bugs crawled past him slower than he was.

And big black violets stared him right in the face with yellow violet eyes.

Starflowers bloomed over his head, and wild parsley and thyme, in this world of once upon a time when one bird sang for him alone.

And he went on and on in this wonderful world he had never seen before. Past a big gray stone to a running stream clear and cold to dip his nose in.

What a wonderful world, and the bird still sang.

And the ferns smelled warm at noon.

And he dozed there under a wild geranium that looked like a small wild rose. His pink little ears lay flat on his head, and his whiskers twitched as the bees flew by, and the first butterfly flew out of June and July, in those northern woods so long ago. The Bunny fell asleep. And the shadows grew long, and the Bunny dreamed that the sun would never go down.

Then all at once he woke up!

He was alone!

Who was he?

What was he?

O bigger than a bug and smaller than a fern, you are lost!

O best loved Bunny in all the world. Lost in the cool green woods, and the sun will soon go down.

When the Bunny knew this, he jumped inside. Suddenly the world seemed very big and he seemed very little in it.

The Bunny ran into a green grass field.

But the sky was too big there.

He put his paws in the crystal stream.

But the water was too cold there.

He even jumped into the air.

But there was no ground there.

So he ran away.

And then he came back again.

And then he sat there.

He was lost.

He looked high above him, way up the long green stems.

What should he do now?

He twitched his nose.
He dangled his paws.
He flopped his ears.
He leaped in the air.

And then he thumped his hind legs bang on the ground. *Thump—Bang!* the sound echoed through the woods.

And soon, O best loved Bunny in all the world, his big warm mother came running to the side of her lost little Bunny and he wasn't lost anymore.

She took him home to his hollow tree and there she warmed him, the best loved Bunny in all the world. Warm and safe and warm.

And above in the night the winds blew all night long. The winds blew their dark night song across the world at night. Down the valleys they come far away and they blow far away down the valleys where no winds stay for long. And that is the sadness of their wind-blown song. Not for long, never for long. O best loved Bunny in all the world.

THE SNOWSHOE RABBIT

The Snowshoe Rabbit, white as white,
Runs over the snow in the bright moonlight
Invisible on the snow-white hill
As the snow falls down until
The Snowshoe Rabbit runs around
Brown as the leaves
    on the old brown ground
And no one can see him
    running around
Brown as the leaves
    all over the ground.

A BIG WHITE POWDERY WALK

By the dark gray river in the
    soft white snow
I caught a little Rabbit and let him go
Bounding deep in the deep soft snow.

THE FIRST SNOWDROP

Long before the robin dares
To flick his shadow across
 the ground,
When the roots are still asleep
And the cold winds creep
Over the cold still ground,
Suddenly among the leaves
Frail as air, yet
Bolder than a polar bear,
 You will find
 The first snowdrop,
 Long before spring,
 Long before anything
 White and green
 Blooming there.

RABBIT DREAM

Dream of a world as white as snow
Where little Rabbit footprints go
Hopping through the powdery snow,
Powdery snow, powdery snow, whoa!

7 LITTLE HOPTOADS

SEVEN very little hoptoads went out for a hop all on a summer's day.

The first little hoptoad saw a big warm gray shadow. The second little hoptoad saw a big white animal with whiskers. The third little hoptoad saw two red shiny eyes and a short tail. The fourth little hoptoad saw two long soft ears. The fifth little hoptoad saw a little pink nose twitching. The sixth little hoptoad saw little white teeth nibbling a lettuce leaf. The seventh little hoptoad saw a bunny.

Then the seven little hoptoads hopped home to their home, all on a summer's day. They lived in a stump.

FIRE!
FIRE!
FIRE!

"Fire! Fire! Fire!"
shouted Silly Bunny.
"Fire! Fire! Fire!"
The leaves in the woods
were all blazing red.
Silly Bunny thought they were on fire.

"Boo!" said the red squirrel.
"Nuts, nuts, nuts, Silly Bunny!
The woods are not on fire. This is the
Fall of the year. Nuts fall down in the
Fall of the year. Leaves turn red in
the Fall of the year. Nuts, nuts, nuts."

Silly Bunny went down the road till
he came to the garden.
In the garden the flowers were
blazing red.

"Fire! Fire! Fire!" shouted Silly Bunny.
"Fire! Fire! Fire! The garden is on fire!
All the flowers are blazing red."

"Buzz, buzz, buzz,"
said the bee.
"The garden is not on fire.
Buzz, buzz, buzz.
Red flowers bloom in the Fall
of the year. Blazing red flowers
bloom and bloom. Buzz, buzz, buzz."

So Silly Bunny hopped up to the
garden wall.
The sun was going down.
"Fire! Fire! Fire!" shouted Silly Bunny.
"The sun is on fire!"

"Who, who who," said a sleepy old owl.
"Who woke me up?"
"Fire! Fire! Fire!" shouted Silly Bunny.
"The sun is on fire! The sun is
blazing red."
"Who, who, who," said the sleepy old owl.
"You woke me up.
The sun is not on fire.
The sun is going down.
The sun is blazing red
When the sun goes down.
Go to sleep, Silly Bunny."

So Silly Bunny, who was sleepy,
Went to sleep.
But the crickets woke him up.

All at once a big red ball of fire
    blazed in his face.
It was the moon.
"Fire! Fire! Fire!"
    called Silly Bunny.
"The moon is on fire!"

"Full moon, full moon,"
    chirped the crickets.
"Full moon, full moon,
The moon is full
In the Fall of the year,
In the Fall of the year.
The moon is full,
The moon is full
In the Fall of the year,
In the Fall of the year.
The moon is full
And the moon is red."

"Oh, dear," said Silly Bunny.
"I wish there was a fire.
I am getting cold."
And just then he saw a fire burning
    in the woods. Some children were
    cooking marshmallows.
And he went and sat by it.
"Fire! Fire! Fire!" shouted Silly Bunny.
"Yes," said the children.
"Come and warm yourself at our fire."

MISTER DOG

Once upon a time there was a funny dog named Crispin's Crispian. He was named Crispin's Crispian because—

he belonged to himself.

In the mornings, he woke himself up and he went to the icebox and gave himself some bread and milk. He was a funny old dog. He liked strawberries.

POP
POP
COOKIES
SALT

Then he took himself for a walk. And he went wherever he wanted to go.

But one morning he didn't know where he wanted to go.

"Just walk and sooner or later you'll get somewhere," he said to himself.

Soon he came to a country where there were lots of dogs. They barked at him and he barked back. Then they all played together.

But he still wanted to go somewhere, so he walked on until he came to a country where there were lots of cats and rabbits.

The cats and rabbits jumped in the air and ran. So Crispian jumped in the air and ran after them.

He didn't catch them because he ran bang into a little boy.

"Who are you and who do you belong to?" asked the little boy.

"I am Crispin's Crispian and I belong to myself," said Crispian. "Who and what are you?"

"I am a boy," said the boy, "and I belong to myself."

"I am so glad," said Crispin's Crispian. "Come and live with me."

Then they went to a butcher shop—"to get his poor dog a bone," Crispian said.

Now, since Crispin's Crispian belonged to himself, he gave himself the bone and trotted home with it.

And the boy's little boy bought a big lamb chop and a bright green vegetable and trotted home with Crispin's Crispian.

Crispin's Crispian lived in a two-story doghouse in a garden. And in his two-story doghouse, he had a little fur living room with a warm fire that crackled all winter and went out in the summer.

His house was always warm. His house had a chimney for the smoke to go out. And upstairs there was a little bedroom with a bed in it and a place for his leash and a pillow under which he hid his bones.

And there was plenty of room in his house for the boy to live there with him.

S E W N

Crispian had a little kitchen upstairs in his two-story doghouse where he fixed himself a good dinner three times a day because he liked to eat. He liked steaks and chops and roast beef and chopped meat and raw eggs.

This evening he made a bone soup with lots of meat in it. He gave some to the boy, and the boy liked it. The boy didn't give Crispian his chop bone, but he put some of his bright green vegetable in the soup.

And what did Crispian do with his dinner?

Did he put it in his stomach?

Yes, indeed.

He chewed it up and swallowed it into his little fat stomach.

And what did the little boy do with his dinner?
Did he put it in his stomach?
Yes, indeed.
He chewed it up and swallowed it into his little fat stomach.

Crispin's Crispian was a *conservative*.
He liked everything at the right time—
dinner at dinner time,
lunch at lunchtime,
breakfast in time for breakfast,
and sunrise at sunrise,
and sunset at sunset.
And at bedtime—
At bedtime, he liked everything in its
own place—
the cup in the saucer,
the chair under the table,
the stars in the heavens,
the moon in the sky,
and himself in his own little bed.

And then what did he do?

Then he curled in a warm little heap and went to sleep. And he dreamed his own dreams.

That was what the dog who belonged to himself did.

And what did the boy who belonged to himself do?

The boy who belonged to himself curled in a warm little heap and went to sleep. And he dreamed his own dreams.

That was what the boy who belonged to himself did.

GOOD NIGHT
AND
SWEET DREAMS.

HOME FOR A BUNNY

"Spring, Spring, Spring!"
sang the frog.
"Spring!" said the groundhog.

"Spring, Spring, Spring!"
sang the robin.

It was Spring.

The leaves burst out.

The flowers burst out.

And robins burst out of their eggs.

It was Spring.

In the Spring a bunny
came down the road.
He was going to find
a home of his own.
A home for a bunny,
A home of his own,
Under a rock,
Under a stone,
Under a log,
Or under the ground.
Where would a bunny find a home?

“Where is your home?”
he asked the robin.

"Here, here, here,"
sang the robin.
"Here in this nest is my home."

"Here, here, here,"
sang the little robins who were
about to fall out of the nest.
"Here is our home."

"Not for me," said the bunny.
"I would fall out of a nest.
I would fall on the ground."

So he went on
looking for a home.
"Where is your home?"
he asked a frog.

"Wog, wog, wog,"
sang the frog.
"Wog, wog, wog,
Under the water,
Down in the bog."
"Not for me,"
said the bunny.
"Under the water,
I would drown in a bog."

So he went on
looking for a home.
"Where do you live?"
he asked the groundhog.
"In a log," said the groundhog.
"Can I come in?" said the bunny.
"No, you can't come in my log,"
said the groundhog.

So the bunny went down the road.
Down the road
and down the road he went.
He was going to find
a home of his own.
A home for a bunny,
A home of his own,
Under a rock
Or a log
Or a stone.
Where would a bunny find a home?

Down the road
and down the road
and down the road
he went, until—

He met a bunny.
"Where is your home?"
he asked the bunny.

"Here," said the bunny.
"Here is my home.
Under this rock,
Under this stone,
Down under the ground,
Here is my home."

"Can I come in?"
said the bunny.
"Yes," said the bunny.
And so he did.

And that was his home.

THE BRAVE LIFE SAVER

Every Sunday morning the Little Fat Policeman took it easy. His wife shined his badge.

He liked to smoke his pipe and read his paper and take his wife out for a walk.

One Sunday the sun was shining brightly.

The birds were singing sweetly.

The Little Fat Policeman and his wife walked beside the ocean on the yellow sand. There were people lying on the beach. There were people swimming in the green sea. The Little Fat Policeman was eating a peach, when suddenly there was a dreadful yell:

The Little Fat Policeman saw a man who couldn't swim rolling in the waves.

As quick as a wink, before the man could sink, the Little Fat Policeman threw off his blue coat, kicked off his boots, threw down his cap, and ran. Down the beach he ran and took a dive into the waves.

And he dove and swam and kicked and splashed through the great, green, curling ocean.

The man kept bobbing up and down ahead of him and floating out to sea.

The Little Fat Policeman had learned how to rescue people when he went to policeman's school, so he knew what to do. He grabbed the man by the top of his head.

He pulled him by the hair, and swam with him up great, green waves, like mountains in the sea, until he swam safely back to shore.

The Little Fat Policeman's wife danced with joy. She danced upon the yellow sand. And all the people from the beach made a tremendous crowd. They shouted three hurrahs:

"Hurrah!
Hurrah!
Hurrah!
For the Little Fat Policeman,
The finest cop of all!"

And a little boy sang:

"Yo-ho-ho
Yes-sir-ree
O Policeman,
Please save me."

THE LITTLE POLICEMAN

With stiff rhythm *Music by Alec Wilder*

2. One Policeman all alone
In his round house
With his phone.
Ting-ling-ling
Rings in his ear—
This Policeman's always near.
Yo-ho-ho!
Yes-sir-ee!
O Policeman,
Please save me.

3. One Policeman on the beach
Keeps his feet dry,
Eats his peach.
Help! Help! Help!
Now don't you fear—
This Policeman's always near.
Yo-ho-ho!
Yes-sir-ee!
O Policeman,
Please save me.

THE WHISPERING RABBIT

ONCE there was a sleepy little rabbit
Who began to yawn—
And he yawned and he yawned and he yawned and he yawned and he yawned,
"Hmmm————"

He opened his little rabbit mouth when he yawned till you could see his white front teeth and his little round pink mouth, and he yawned and he yawned until suddenly a bee flew into his mouth and he swallowed the bee.

"Hooo—hooo—," said a fat old owl. "Always keep your paw in front of your mouth when you yawn," hooted the owl.

"Rabbits never do that," said the sleepy little rabbit.

"Silly rabbits!" said the owl, and he flew away.

The little rabbit was just calling after him, but when the little rabbit opened his mouth to speak, the bumblebee had curled up to sleep in his throat——AND——all he could do was whisper.

"What shall I do?" he whispered to a squirrel who wasn't sleepy.

"Wake him up," said the squirrel. "Wake up the bumblebee."

"How?" whispered the rabbit. "All I can do is whisper and I'm sleepy and I want to go to sleep and who can sleep with a bumblebee—"

Suddenly a wise old groundhog popped up out of the ground.

"All I can do is whisper," said the little rabbit.

"All the better," said the groundhog.

"Come here, little rabbit," he said, "and I will whisper to you how to wake up a bumblebee.

"You have to make the littlest noise that you can possibly make because a bumblebee doesn't bother about big noises. He is a very little bee and he is only interested in little noises."

"Like a loud whisper?" asked the rabbit.

"Too loud," said the groundhog, and popped back into his hole.

"A little noise," whispered the rabbit, and he started making little rabbit noises—he made a noise as quiet as the sound of a bird's wing cutting the air, but the bee didn't wake up. So the little rabbit made the sound of snow falling, but the bee didn't wake up.

So thc little rabbit made the sound of a bug breathing and a fly sneezing and grass rustling and a fireman thinking. Still the bee didn't wake up. So the rabbit sat and thought of all the little sounds he could think of—What could they be?

A sound quiet as snow melting, quiet as a flower growing, quiet as an egg, quiet as—And suddenly he knew the little noise that he would make—and he made it.

It was like a little click made hundreds of miles away by a bumblebee in an apple tree in full bloom on a mountaintop. It was the very small click of a bee swallowing some honey from an apple blossom.

And at that the bee woke up.

He thought he was missing something and away he flew.

And then what did the little rabbit do? That sleepy sleepy little rabbit?

He closed his mouth
He closed his eyes
He closed his ears
And he tucked in his paws
And twitched his nose
And he went sound asleep!

I LIKE CARS

Red cars Green cars

Sport limousine cars

I like cars
A car in a garage
A car with a load
A car with a flat tire
A car on the road
I like cars.

TOURS
HILL
STOP

STARSHIP

I LIKE STARS

Yellow stars
Green stars
Red stars
Blue stars
I like stars
Far stars
Quiet stars
Bright stars
Light stars
I like stars
A star that is shooting across the dark sky
A star that is shining right straight in your eye
I like stars.

Little Golden Books
Little Golden Books
Little Golden Books
Little Golden Books
Little Golden Books
Little Golden Books